# REALISATION OF TRUTH

(LAGHUKATHA SANGRAH)

DR DINESH PATHAK SHASHI

DEDICATED

TO

Dr.Maharaj Krishn Jain.

# Contents

# Contents

# Foreword

## SHORT STORIES -TORCH BEARER OF SOCIETY

Realisation of truth is the self-proof of consciousness or awareness prevalent in the society. Conscious intellectual is enlightened with his deeds moving above the material pleasure and keeps on challenging the darkness all around. All these challenges are coming before us through the short stories collection of Dr Dinesh Shashi Pathak.

This is his second short story collection.Before this his first short story collection was published in 2000. This is the first chance when I have got the opportunity to read his short story.While reading these stories, I have realised that he moves your pen only after understanding the utility of literature.

His stories deal with every class of the society. The diction of the stories is very clear and lofty in other words the stories in this collection which are full of all the nine senses presents the truth and unity of composition defines the coolness of the collection

The very first story of this collection ' Victory ' makes us realise that it is a wide description on relation. There is a chastity of relation between men and women.Trust and loyalty provides a positive direction to human life. The short story 'Regret' is the story of prejudice of old parents. The central theme of the story is expectations from son & daughter – in- law disappointing circumstances created due to this The relations in the story get a positive direction at last , struggling with life's condition. This is a very nice short story which points out the infected opinions due to misunderstanding.

The tyrannical behaviours of the police in the story " Listen , King Bhoj " is enough to move our heart and mind. Dr Dinesh Pathak Shashi very well throws light on every class of society the government officials , evil systems etc. The short story " Status Quo " has pointed out the polities played by different political party to name a crossroad.

Naming of the crossroad as 'Parashuram crossroad' presenting the foolish mentality of society creates a chaos in the mind and heart. Family problem like the relations between siblings, the outburst of TTE in the train , satire of the co-passengers is very well expressed in ' parallel pain '.

In the story ' service ' the protagonist is a government servant. He wants to be transferred to his desired place. Otherwise, he tries to get it held back and for this purpose he does not hesitate to misuse the name of his old parents and after accomplishment of his purpose he goes to a hill station, with his family.

This is his service feeling for his parents. Reading this story many questions are arising in mind. What is the culture of the family? How will their children, behave with them in the future? In the story 'Shadow' the son becomes sad. On the death his mother, who was of 105 years old. His responsibility as the main member of the family reveals a new experiment of language . The short story "The truth of life" the questions put up by a small child and answers given by his grandfather with reference to spring and autumn season, makes this story worthy to read. Such matters should be discussed by the writes. Similarly : Guardian, Hope, Calm, Your, My and his house, answer, desire, beggar, obligation : give us a message of nature, married life, doctor's advise after operation and life of the prisoners reveal a new creativity.

As we all know that sentiments and passion have more importance than the style, that takes the readers to the outside world. In the present time the scene of short story is undergoing changes. Some years ago, the writers hesitated to discuss this genre of literature, today it is a matter of discussion in almost all the institutions of literature. The writer must not think about what the reader would like to read. I hope Dinesh Shashi Pathak will also agree with my opinion. Writer should keep in mind what he wants the readers to read. the writer should see how the literature should be promoted and should be made interesting. They should think how the society will improve.He should think how the compositions are presented in order to increase the interest of readers in reading books. These short stories reflect the same thing. These stories read our mind..

It's an untold fact that the expressed feelings are the strong wishes of a person and only these feelings keep them secure. The short stories compel us to feel the heart although partially. Many of these stories are very strong in style and plot. Even though his stories are of all time, they have not got place as the deserved. It is my moral duty to express my regret on this.

A writer always suffers from many difficulties. Dr Dinesh Pathak is one if such writers. His knowledge and thought, is like an award in Hindi literature.

The writer has lived in various aspects of life, being a government servant in railway as an engineer and established in the soil of Braj. His writings are like the rainbow in the sky. May God bless him with higher success in the field of literature.

With best wishes.

Miss Kanta Roy

Administrative Officer
Hindi Bhavan, Bhopal (460002)
Short story research centre
Bhopal
Chief editor, Short story circle
Mob : 9575465147

# Preface

## REALISATION OF TRUTH --Short stories with a reference to society and family.

I have received the second collection of short stories of the established writer Dr Dinesh Pathak Shashi. Dr Dinesh Pathak has been awarded with many respectable Awards hence we find matured thought and experience of life. Along with his sentimental consciousness he is a very widely read writer and his stories reveal every class of the society. Various factors of family life have been embedded in his short stories like Shadow, Truth of Life, Calm, desire, Answer, Fate etc.

' Truth of life is a sensitive short story in which a child asks the reason why plants get dried after bearing fruits. Eyes of the grandfather in the story gets wet giving answer to his question, " So that new sapling might grow up, my child. " The story ' superior-Inferior' establishes the fact that superior is always superior. " Fate " portrays the boundation of the hero. His desire to eat food prepared by daughters-in-law remained a dream and he started to search a maid servant.

Similarly, there are many short stories which enlighten our path like the pole star, like – Parallel Pain, Corona will be defeated. In the latter one the mistress of the family gives advance payment to the maid and instructs her not to come out of the house in corona curfew ' service feeling ' is about a pseud who gets his transfer halted taking excuse of his parent's care and then goes to hill station with his family. It is a satire on the negligent attitude of children towards their parent's and how they use their elders for their personal advantage.

In this story collection the writer has expressed thediscrepancies in the administration. In the story 'Listen, King Bhoj' the writer has highlighted the working pattern of the police. The story 'Guardian' reveals the corruption prevalent in government offices. The local colour added according to the character enhances the beauty of the story. The story 'Status Quo' is about the politicians and flatterers who are after changing the name of crossroad for their vote bank.

Many stories related to corruption draw our attention like- Protection money, Anti-corruption. 'Hope' story is a philosophical one. Sudden clouds make the hero gloomy but immediately when the weather becomes clear, he gets a new energy.

Child psychology is very well expressed in his short story, 'I know them'Nikhil in this story feels bad when his parents criticize his grandparents, children are very innocent. They move where they get love.

'Inner conflict' has very efficiently described the psychology of a lady. Mother under work pressure beats her daughter badly and when interfered by her father-in-law, weeps bitterly and wishes for the service of her husband.

The writer has used a very lofty language in 'Courtesy'. Here the daughter-in-law refuses tea to her father-in-law and whenher husband demands she immediately agrees and goes to the kitchen to prepare tea. This story expresses the sentiments towards the old people.

Several short stories of this collection are very short, only of two to four lines like- honesty target , lesson, law, etc. 'Who is innocent?' is a satire. While'lesson',' Honesty', ' service' are some where the writer has made a very good use of idioms.

The stories are very simple and smooth from the point of view of style and Art of writing.

I have full faith that this short story collection of Dr. Dinesh Pathak will be adored by the readers. Many congratulations to Dr. Dinesh Pathak 'Shashi' for this collection.

With best wishes<br>
Dr. Sheel Kaushik<br>
(Awarded the best women writer by<br>
Haryana Sahitya Academy)<br>
Major house-17, Hudda, sector- 20<br>
Part-1, Sirsa, 125056, Haryana<br>
Mobile no.- 94168-47107

# Acknowledgements

## FROM WRITER'S PEN

It's my belief that no genre of literature is possible by making special efforts. Feelings emerge in the heart of a writer only by the grace of Godess Saraswati, and his pen moves naturally without making any effort. Maybe this is not applicable to all writers but I have myself experienced all these things myself. If this were not a fact, my 1st short story was published in 2000 and after that it took 22 years for my second short story collection to be published .In between these years, I was successful in getting several stories, children's stories, children's novel, drama, satire, biographies and criticisms published, about 30-35 books in various genre.

Truly speaking, the work of writing short stories is not so easy as people take it.

Two very wise and learned writers have written the preface of this short story collection. Preface has been written by miss Kanta Roy, the director of short story research centre, Bhopal and editor too. She also administrative officer of Hindi Bhavan, Bhopal. Even after so many responsibilities, she gave her precious time to write the preface of my collection. I thank her from the core of my heart.

I am heartily obliged to Dr Sheel Kaushik too, for writing the 2nd preface for my collection. Dr Sheel Kaushik was awarded as best writer by Haryana Sahitya Academy. She is successful doctor by profession.

In some way or other my wife, Smt. Shashi, my sons, Akash and Sagar, both my daughters-in-law, Anupama and Sanika, grandson Saksham and other family members have also extended their support in writing this collection. Writers of Mathura, Dr Neeraj Shastri, Mr Jitendra Vimal, Mr Madan Mohan Sharma "Arvind". I am thankful to Mrs Vandana Asthana for translating the short story collection into English. To thank all these personalities is my moral duty.

I am thankful to the owner and authorities of the Notion press, Chennai for publishing this collection and giving it a proper platform.

This collection is the result of my experience and feelings. If you also feel the same things happening around you, then I will think that my toil was not a waste. Yours

Dr Dinesh Pathak 'Shashi'
28, SARANG VIHAR Mathura-6,
mob.-9870631805
E-mail- drdinesh57@gmail.com

CHAPTER ONE

# VICTORY

He is a man.

And she is a woman.

The woman looked into the eyes of the man and was spell bounded. Finding a secret and proper place , she invited the man.

Come on let's enjoy the pleasure of life completely. Perhaps nature has brought both of us here for this only.

No, I am already in commitment with someone else. The man smiled looking at the princess of beauty.

Hearing the answer, the woman gazed at him with surprise. Such behaviour of the man was incredulous and unexpected to the woman. Pinching her hand she tried to find out if she were dreaming.

Even today I am happy to accept my defeat, man,because in this case also woman has triumphed.Victory of a woman for the first time. Victory of your wife.

CHAPTER TWO

# TRUTH OF LIFE

On the weekend, since morning I had started uprooting the dry plants of poppy flowers of my garden. With the passage of time, the colourful poppy plants which had dried, used to spread their pleasant beauty throughout the lawn sometimes ago.

"Papa, now our lawn is looking so beautiful. The old and dried plants had covered these beautiful new flowers. Isn't it papa?"

"Yes, my dear! Spring follows autumn and autumn follows spring. This is the law of nature."

"But father, why do these beautiful flowers dry up? Why don't they always remain blooming?"

I was going to tell him the scientific reason of drying plants when my old father sitting there at some distance on a cot, called him.

"Come here, I will tell you the reason why they dry up." The child rushed towards grandfather.

"Yes grandfather, tell me."

"So that new flowers get a chance to come."

He patted on the child's head and his eyes became tearful. That small child was puzzled, why grandfather became so emotional giving such a small answer.

CHAPTER THREE

# REGRET

Daughter-in-law never leaves an opportunity of going to her parents' house. She forced her husband to take her with him and drop her at her parent's house. I always felt it though I was not aware of the reality.

I was surprised to think that even her parents did not instruct her that now her real home is her in-laws house and in addition to it her old mother-in-law needs her utmost care. They perhaps never think about her duty towards her in-laws.

Several times I got very disappointed. I went inside the kitchen and started washing the dishes, cooking food and feeding my wife, giving her medicine and then used to go to office. but sometimes I used to be very disappointed. I kept thinking if I had given birth to my child for this day. Such irresponsible daughter-in-law in my luck.

One day I came to know that their office was off. I thought they would get up at 9 o'clock. But to my surprise, I saw them awaken at 5 o'clock and were getting ready to go somewhere. I asked my son, where they were going.

"Yes, we are going to Delhi."

"And your wife?"

"She too." He answered shortly.

"And your child? Are you taking him also?"

"We shall leave him in her maternal grandmother's house, on the way."

I was very irritated but remained silent as I did not want that their journey should start in tension.

They returned with 2 bags full in the evening as if they had gone for shopping.

Daughter-in-law took out one piece sleeping suit and put it on the child's body. She pushed the chain and made him stand. The dress was so tight that it troubled me so much. He was not even able to stand properly.

I could not resist myself and spoke out. This suit is too tight for the child.

But she was not ready to accept and said, "No, father. This is a sleeping suit. It is worn like this only."

But I grew more angry and took out the clothes from his body and threw away.

"Yes, I don't know anything. My whole life passed in innocence. Only you know everything."

She too got frightened with these words, but said nothing. The next day, when she saw me silent, she came with the shopping bags and showed the clothes she had brought for me, her mother-in-law and brother-in-law.

After seeing the empty bag in her hands,I asked, "What did you both bring for yourself?"

"No, father. We have many clothes. Recently they are not needed to us. I was thinking of bringing these clothes for you but was not getting time. Yesterday, we got time, so we went to market."

I was surprised. Our daughter in law cares so much about us but we have never tried to understand her. I regreted on my anger shown the previous day.

CHAPTER FOUR

# SERVICE

Being a government servant, he was transferred from place to place but he always chose the place of his liking by making efforts.

But this time, he was transferred to an unexpected place. As usual he tried to get place of his choice, but did not succeed. The senior officer being honest there was no chance of bribing too. He was much worried. he was not finding any solution to his problem and sat disappointedly. His wife too became anxious and tried to console him.

"Don't take tension. Take leave for some days. Let us go to our village for some days. You will get relaxed and children will spend time with grandparents. In every letter they complain that we do not go to village. They will also feel happy."

Wife's opinion gave him an idea. He looked at his wife with appraisal and started drafting a letter-

"Sir,

My parents are very old and there is no one except me to look after them. So, it's my sincere request not to send me away from my village."

He was successful in his target. Returning from office, there was a look of triumph on his face. He declared this good news before his wife. "I have succeeded" and started planning to go to some hill station during the holidays.

The letter of old parents fell down from the tableand no one noticed.

CHAPTER FIVE

# LISTEN, KING BHOJ

He was proud of the police department of his kingdom for the peaceful arrangement they made in the kingdom. He praised them whenever he got the opportunity. Still he regreted whenever there was any incident of robbery, theft etc... He thought, how it became possible Inspite of alert police department.

He was never ready to accept anything spoken against the police department. People tried to convince him that it was not 'Stayug' and police itself is involved in crimes, he got angry.

But one day, an incident broke his faith. One day a robber broke into his house. He was in drunk condition. He created a great chaos in the house. when he saw all this after returning from office, he reached the local police post and informed everything to the inspector.

But something strange happened. The inspector got him locked up ordering a constable.

He was amazed at that behaviour of police officer. He tried to give clarification that some other person and not he was the culprit. But police was not ready to listen anything. In the morning he was taken to the court.

He protested saying that he couldn't be kept in lockup without informing any family member, but police did not give ear to whatever he said. All his knowledge was kept aside.

He had now realised that all the rules and regulations were of no use before these corrupt police officers. His faith on the department had broken and scattered like pieces of glass.

The inspector, the constable and the whole police station seemed like a gathering of robbers and thieves.

CHAPTER SIX

# STATUS QUO

There was a big crowd within no time. The political leader was trying to exploit the religious emotions of the people and the crowd soon converted into a procession. Everyone was shouting a single slogan- “Name this crossroad—Parashuram Crossroad in place of bank crossroad”

Some people in the procession were destroying the public property while some were sitting on hunger strike. There was a big jam o the road due to a long queue of vehicles.

Police van came giving loud sirens. They fired in the air to frighten the crowd. And there was lathi charge also. Many people were badly wounded and were admitted in the hospital. There was blood all around.

But the public did not care the for the dying people. They just wanted to get the crossroad name changed to ‘Parashuram crossroad’ on the name of their Saint Parashuram. The political leader provoked the people to shout slogan.

As a consequence the leader was arrested and sent to jail. Public had sympathy wave for the leader that he had gone jail due to them. Thus it was quite impossible for them to deceive their leader.

The flatterers of the leader cried the slogan in louder voice and sat on a strike on crossroad along with the crowd.

The strike continued for some days and at last their demand was fulfilled.

Public was happy with changed name of crossroad. That leader got sympathy of people and won election.

His supporters too were happy as they were expecting their shares in 5 lakh rupees given to them.

Everyone except the statue of saint Parashuram was happy. Tears were continuously flowing from eyes of the statue of Parashuram. It was troubled with pollution all around and the dirt of the birds sitting on the head of the statue.

The leader won the election but people remained in the same condition. Nothing except the name of the crossroad changed.

It was all status quo.

CHAPTER SEVEN

# SUPERIOR-INFERIOR

We were expecting myelder brother in a marriage where we too had to go. His wife often discussed the cleverness and playful activities ofGuddan , her two year old child. My wife too used to talk about our one and half years old son , babu. They used to discuss these things on phone.

This was the first time when these two children will get the opportunity to meet each other. My wife started training our child , how he had to beat his sister and not to remain introvertly. They will see which of the two child is more playful.

The small child acted in the same way , as we told , raising his hand , that it looked so funny and both of us laughed and my wife felt proud of her son.

As soon as we reached the marriage home my wife asked “babu “ to move forward and meet her sister. ‘ The boy immediately pushed her and sat over her. All the relatives laughed at the activity while my wife was smiling proudly and said , “ Sister you always used to say that guddan is very active but she -------”

Seeing his daughter frightening brother said , Oh ! your Babu is really very naughty. When we talked on telephone. I always thought that he is not so naughty as guddan, sister – in – law too supported him.

After the programme ended, we made preparation to come back. Just then sister-in-law took out a very beautiful toy and a pair of dress. She handed it to Rashmi , saying that it was for ' Babu '. They had bought it from Meerut.

Both of us felt embarrassedat this as we had brought nothing for their daughter. We also should have thought of bringing something for Guddan. We were busy in training our son how to defeat his sister in cleverness and playful.

I felt people who are great are always noble in their behaviour and those who are trivial and narrowminded always remain inferior in their behaviours. We were feeling ourselves dwarf before the greatness of brother and sister – in – law.

CHAPTER EIGHT

# Parallel Pain

The young man showed two tickets to the T.T.E , as soon as the latter demanded.

"The ticket is for general compartment." The ticket checker told the lady sitting with her and asked the passenger sitting on the corner to move aside and he sat on the seat.

" Yes ---- Yes , actually we caught the train in a hurry. So could not get into the proper coach. Our going was very urgent , Sir " the young man gave explanation.

" Give one hundred seventy-two rupees "

As soon as the T.T.E. opened the receipt book for charging the fine , the young man expressed his helplessness in giving the money.

" If you had no money , why did you get into the coach ? "

At this insulting rebuke the young man handed 80 rupees to him. At first the T.T.E counted the money suddenly , then started counting it loudly and said , " These are only 80 rupees. I cannot even make receipt out of this money "

Saying this he got up with a start and moved towards another coach.

The lady with him whispered to the young man and at her indication he moved towards the TTE.

He came back after an hour. Their one fourth journey was over. He sat for some time , but was very worried. He again got up and went towards the TTE.

When he returned this time they had covered half the distance. Ultimately when journey of 4 to 5 Kms was left TTE was seen coming with the young man.

The man looked very worried and tried because he had been running after the TTE again and again. And latter threatened him but was not giving him receipt.

The lady was watching everything silently. There was a mixed reaction of the co-passengers in the compartment. Some were happy on their condition ; some others were advising to travel with tickets while some others were looking at him with suspicion.

" If they have eloped from somewhere " some people were passing satires at the lady.

The young man was growing more and more anxious while the lady was still silent.

As their station was about to come TTE asked the young man.

"Now give me , what you have. "

The man handed him the folded notes in his hand and felt relief.

TTE , reminding of the favours conferred , advised the young man , then suddenly he remembered. Something and smiling satirically he asked him,

" By the way , where are you going ? what is the urgent work for which you are going ?"

some of the passengers laughed, " They are going to enjoy , what can be more urgent than this work " one of the passengers blew whistle. That young lady stared those passengers and broke out weeping.

" Yes , I am going to enjoy , you also go to enjoy with your sister when your father dies. "

There was silence all around every one tried to escape everyone's eyes TTE put his hands in his pocket and taking out the money gave if to the young man saying " keep itif may be of same use to you. "

Then he looked at the lady saying " excuse me sister " and moved in the other coach with bend head.

Perhaps some past moment made them partners in their sorrow as if both were standing in the same court.

CHAPTER NINE

# SHADOW

Ill health of grandmother had made her Peevish. Her nature was becoming intolerable for the family members.

She irritated not only family members but also neighbours. No one wanted to sit with her and used to comment.

" This old lady has drunk immortal drink. Till when she will live in this world. She is one hundred and five years old now. "

Women from the neighbourhood never forget to express their views.She repeated the same thing many times , chhutka spoke out being irritated " Oh ! grandmother , why do you repeat the same thing. you just don't have patience and you make a hue and cry in the house.

The whole night she keptcalling loudly and disturbed everyone's sleep but Inspite of all this, father remained silent and peaceful and served her the whole night. He was never irritated by her continuous cry , disturbing his sleep or her childlike importunity.

One day grandmother left us and this world. Father sank into deep silence. I could not tolerate his silence.

" Why are you so silent papa. After all grandmother was one hundred and five years old. You did your best and served her with full devotion every son cannot do this. Then why are you so regretful ? "

Father broke the silence "You are right son. But I always felt a shadow above my head as long as she was alive, I felt myself like a small child before her but now , when she is no more , I have become the head of the family how peaceful we feel. When shadow of our elders remain over our head ! you will understand it only after me. "

CHAPTER TEN

# GUARDIAN

I gave signal with my hand for the truck to stop , when I got tired of waiting for the bus for two hours. The distance of my destination was only forty kms.

The truck had hardly moved a distance of 10 kms when the checking jeep stopped the truck.

I grew suspicious that they might stop the truck for long hours. They might check every packet in the truck. I was also fearful if there wereany illegal things in the truck like drugs , opium or any smuggling material. I thought I might be late in reaching.

On the one hand I was getting irritated for getting late on the other hand I was happy to see that our security is so strong and active that people cannot do any kind of illegal activities.

I was in a deep thought when a constable came and stood before the truck. The truck driver abused him and gave 50 rupees note in his hand.

"Give some more " demanded the constable.

" You idiots come and stand in our way. " The driver abused him badly and handed him one more note of 50 rupees. "

The constable moved towards the other truck , keeping the 50 rupees note in the pocket. I could not stop myself and asked , " Constable kept the money in his pocket. He did not give you any receipt"

At this the driver laughed saying , " If he has not given me any receipt its well , I have no receipt of all the goods loaded in this truck. If I can make a profit of thousands of rupees by giving hundred rupees , what's the loss. "

" But , are you not afraid of driving a truck with illegal things ? "

" What is there to fear , if we have protectors , gunners at every step where shall we get such a great profit by sacrificing one hundred rupees. Sometimes when we get some very honest person like Satyavadi Harish Chandra , we have to face problem. "

He shared his experience in a high spirit.

CHAPTER ELEVEN

# HOPE

The pleasant sun of winter season suddenly disappeared and there where dark clouds in the sky There was darkness all around and very cool breeze was blowing.

Sunlight and darkness, how similar are the conditions of my life and this weather change. Suddenly my happy and easy going life was surrounded with dark clouds of hardship. Family , relatives all were in pain. Incurable disease had attacked . He was in a difficult situation , neither able to help others nor was able to ask others for help.

Struggling with the difficult situation he started feeling defeated. He sank into depression and became very silent.

He was comparing his life with the changing weather conditions , when suddenly the sun got free from the clutches of dark clouds and there was sun all around.

I too became hopeful. I thought if the dark clouds disappeared and there was sunshine , my trouble will also change into joy one day.

And with this thought there was a hopeful smile on my lips.

CHAPTER TWELVE

# CALM

I was feeling sick.Sickness was growing intensely. I was not at all worried about myself. I knew death is universal truth , what to fear of ! but I was worried about my wife who will be left behind me .Due to bad luck my wife had become deaf and was unable to read and write since many years. In such condition a communication gap developed between wife and children. My son and daughter – in – law could not understand the favour she did to them. That's why they often used to talk with her in an irritable tone , that her eyes used to become teary. Several times she used to weep bitterly when she could not give explanation. Her sentimental situation , provoked my sentiments too. I often got into a dilemma between the behaviour of son & daughter – in – law and innocence of wife and I tried to console my wife and convince son and daughter – in – law to understandher condition.

Whenever I was unable to convince them , my heart wept , thinking what will happen to my wife after me ? How will the children treat her ? Maybe they load her with all the household work. They may torture her in case she failed to perform her work properly. I had never spoken in a loud voice even since my marriage.

Today only she wept bitterly when son told her something. I felt very bad. But now I was feeling so sick that I was helpless.

I was lying on the roof. At night staring at the sky in a worried condition, when I could overhear the conversation going on between son and daughter – in – law. She was telling

" You just tell anything to mother without any pre thinking. Yes, must see that she never faced any trouble in the times of father. If she too suffers from heart attack. We shall become orphan. Shadow of elders is very essential. The protect their children from many odd situations. Don't you ever think about it ? "

I felt a deep relief in my heart hearing her sensible words I thought , now I can die in peace.

CHAPTER THIRTEEN

# YOUR , MY AND HIS HOUSE

As soon as he opened the lunch box during lunch time , he was angry to see pickles in a large quality in one of the containers of the lunch box.

He murmured in himself and reaching the house, started complaining to his wife and took his dinner carelessly.

" Why did you keep so much of pickles in the lunch box. Instead of pickle you could have kept salad – raddish , carrot , beat. "

Wife got irritated –

I have got so much of work. Time is needed to cut salad. How can I get so much time in the morning hours? "

Felt angry and guilty in my mind and thought of the time fifteen years before when we were newly married.

Fifteen years before I used to do job in Delhi. For reaching there I had to start from home at 3 O'clock in the night , to catch train. When he was about to start , he found his lunch box ready.

I looked at her lovingly and used to say " why do you disturb your sleep in the midnight, I can take my lunch in hotel too. "

But she never failed in her duty. " No , I don't feel any trouble. I love working for you. Why do you say like this? "

She looked at him lovingly and gave the dish of his choice in the lunch , every day and he went to office in a happy mood.

But today -------- time has changed a lot. He was amazed how the love between husband and wife reduces with time. Otherwise, his wife world not have answered in such a way.

He went in the other room and laid down on the bed. I was in a sorrow full mood.

" I will not carry lunch box from tomorrow. He turned and tossed. Just then he felt someone's hand on his body. "

" Hello , feeling sleepy ? "

He did not give any answer and kept lying in same position.

" Have this "Carrot Halwa " it is your favourite dessert. I had been thinking to prepare it for long but was not getting time. Don't know how time passes the whole day . "

" I had hidden it for you. You know small children finish everything. "

Hearing her words, he realised the reason of keeping pickles in the lunch box.He looked at his wife's face. Her face seemed very attractive and he could see the same fifteen-year-old love in her eyes.

CHAPTER FOURTEEN

# ANSWER

I was strictly advised by the doctor to lay down flat on the bed without any movement , as I had an operation of prostrate. I was advised to keep my legs , hand and neck still. I could neither speak nor could change my condition for about three to four hours. Time passed , ankles of my feet grew stiff and I felt a heat coming out of it.

Every part of the body was paining. I was suffering from hell like pain. I was afraid , if I made movement, stich might open and the days of suffering might increase. I was tired of tolerating and called my son who was with me in the hospital and told him about my problem.

My son kept ankle heel of one of my legs in his hand. He too was shocked to see the position it was really very hot. He caressed my heels with his cool hands. I felt a bit relaxed. He kept awake the whole night pressed my heels to reduce my problem.

Lying on the bed in the hospital , I suddenly remembered a childhood incident. A contractor from my village was given the contract of making a new building of jail. I was very curious to see that building. To satisfy my childhood curiosity , he took me there and showed the prison building. There were several very tiny constructions in which one could stand but not move one's body or sit in a relaxed posture. I could not resist my curiosity and enquired

"Uncle , why this small construction ? "

Uncle, explained me that wherever a culprit is given a strict punishment he is made to stand in these cells. I did not feel it a difficult task that time and laughed loudly telling , " what's the problem , anybody can stand like this ? "

The restriction suggested by my doctor during these 24 hours gave me the answer to the question I had asked uncle in my childhood. I was craving to move my hands and feet but for the fear of damaging the stiches , I did not dare to move.

I started thinking , nobody should commit such mistake as is bound to suffer in those small cells.

CHAPTER FIFTEEN

# DESIRE

Since my childhood I was taught by my father the custom of touching feet of elder – sister , brother , sister – in – law , neighbour or any other relation whenever I met them.

He taught me to wish with folded hands every known person , I used to meet on the way and in return. I used to get a lot of blessings and their loving hands on my head made me feel very satisfied and peaceful.

With everyone's blessings I grew up and was married to a goddess like girl. By the grace of God, I was blessed with two sons. But perhaps due to some sins of my prebirth. I had to suffer a lot due to my wife's degrading health and had to spend most of my time in hospitals in ICUs. I could not take care of my sons. Rather they themselves helped me in household works.

I could not transfer the culture in my children. Consequently, my younger son did not develop a habit of touching feet of his elder brother and sister-in-law. He felt more comfortable in shaking hands and telling Hai ----- Hello. I never saw my elder son and his wife giving heartly blessings to their younger brother , as I had received from my elders.

I have a deep desire that both my sons should love each other heartily. But their behaviourand attitude towards each other makes me disappointed , but what is my fault ? Shall I be able to get the answer before my death?

CHAPTER SIXTEEN

# BEGGAR

My eyes caught sight of a man with beggar like appearance , who was badly wounded I felt pity and stopping my scooter on the side , I began to observe him minutely. My younger son who was with me that time was also looking at him with amazement.

" Father , he is badly wounded. It seems as if some vehicle has struck him. Blood is flowing from his whole body. Father he will die if he keeps lying here without any treatment. "

I too became emotionalas soon as he looked at me with pity in his eyes. I patted his hand sympathetically people around there smiled at me.

I felt they will be mocking. Nothing strange , because in the present time people think it a foolishness and derision to help any helpless person. But I never care for such people and I decided to take that man to the hospital.

I once again tried to make him stand up holding his hand and asked him to come with me to the hospital.

A policeman , who was looking at me , doing all this , pressed one of his eyes that embarrassed me.

I understood that there was some secretbehind his wounded condition and he was pretending to be in pain. Leaving him I started from there with my son.

My son was surprised at my suddenly changed behaviour. I had no sympathy with him now. But my son was still thinking about that poor man. In the evening when it was a bit dark he two some chapati and 5 rupees from his mother and went to the beggar.

I felt very angry on my son's behaviour certainly the beggar was a fraud. I started murmuring , that's why the policeman had given me a hint.

Now that beggar will blackmail him emotionally and will excite him to bring food and money daily.

With all these thoughts I rushed after my son and reaching there I stood at a hidden place. The beggar was still lying there in the same condition. He called the beggar.

" Baba , take some food , money and medicine. Come I will first clean your wound. "He took out cotton , dettol and some ointment.

The beggar linked at the innocent face of boy and turned his hands on his head.

" No dear , I am not sitting here to cheat innocent children like you. Take your money and medicine back and give it to your parents. This is not blood; this is colour mixed in sugar. "

He told washing the colour from one place. I was bound to think that the beggars are not as they look,

CHAPTER SEVENTEEN

# OBLIGATION

" Listen "

Ramesh looked back in surprise.

Take these 2000 Rupees that you had given me as debt. May God help you to remain Idealist throughout your life. We can't not let you spoil your life worrying about your son. We just wish that you remain like a rosary , guiding us.

This was the voice of madam.

Ramesh was moving in flashback on the advice of office superintendent son Umesh , filled up the form again with the photo copies of all marksheets and bank draft. He did not receive his degree even after two years wait.In the meantime, he completed his post-graduation and applied for the post of P.O. in bank.

He passed the written exam. And the date of interview was announced. He was worried about the interview which was to be conducted two monthslater. He went to Mr Dubey , superintendent of the office and told him everything. Mr. Dubey consoled him that he will send the degree for signature of the registrar and the vice chancellor and within 20 – 25 days he will receive it by post.

After one month when it was not received Ramesh went to Mr Dubey. To know the real condition , he told to meet Mr. O.S.Vikram. He checked the register and said guessing

, " Maybe it is in registrar or V.C. Office for signature. Ramesh told him that the peons do not allow to touch the files. At this Mr. Vikram told him to ask madam at the counter the date of despatch , it will then become easy to find out in the register.

Madam told to spend some money for this work. Mr Ramesh was surprised to hear this.

" I too delivered my service for 37 years but never even tried to take the obligation of a single cup of tea , let alone any bribe. "

" But here peons expect something even when they shift a file from one table to the other. "

Mr Ramesh got emotional but there was no option left. He was compelled to sacrifice his idealism for the future of his son. The fourth day his degree was in his hand.

Ramesh stood with folded hand before madam. His place of idealism was saved from being demolished.

CHAPTER EIGHTEEN

# FATE

Mr Sharma and his wife were very happy hearing the news that all his sons and daughters-in-law are coming on the festival of Holi. They thought they will have the fortune of eating food made by their daughter-in-law. They were tired of eating bread , toast and such other things from market. They were 70-80 years old and thus did not like to cook anything themselves. The empty house also gave a feeling of dullness. Our house will also give a feeling of joy. When children will come and play and jump in the whole house.

Mr Sharma started making a list of things to be brought from the market. So that the children might not face any problem and we don't have to rush for market.

He had just returned from the market with the things of their choice when he received the phone call of elder daughter – in – law.

"Babuji, arrange some maid to cook food on Holi when we come. The whole year we remain busy in our house hold work. We shall also get some rest and will be able to enjoy the festival. Your younger daughter-in-law is also of the same opinion "

Mr Sharma became disappointed he lost the colour of his face. He thought this is the fate of old people and he started looking for a maid to cook food. ***

CHAPTER NINETEEN

# HELPLESSNESS

He was appointed on the post of quality control inspector in a limited company after completing his study of engineering. There he had to do eight hours of inspection on the floor.

After two to three years, he got a government job and hence resigned from the limited company. There he had less work but responsibility of 24 hours he had to be active 24 hours whenever he had to go out. He had to inform his partner as anything goes through breakdown anytime.

Although the office time was 8 AM to 5 PM, he was called anytime in 24 hours in case of failure of any machine and this was frequent. Many times, he had to go at 6 in the morning, many times at 3 AM. There was no fixed time. Thirty years passed this way. Meantime his son and daughters were married and grandchildren had started going to school.

One day his elder daughter-in-law asked him the time of his office. He told her that it was 8 O'clock.

" Then you can take Saksham with you. His school van also comes on the highway at 8 O'clock."

He agreed to the proposal and this routine continue for 2-3 days. Then on the fourth day he was called in the office at 6 O'clock in the morning. So, he could not take his grandson to school. Thenext day also he had to go to office in the midnight at 2 AM and came back at 1pmh and could not perform his duty.

After so many years now he realised that the job of a clerk is better than his job. At least his job is of fixed time. He passed 30 years irregular time schedule. He never realised this irregular routine. He had to work to earn money. Now when his irregular routine stopped him from imparting his duty towards his grandson , he felt that he was helpless. He could not even drop his child to school. He is so powerless ? He thought helplessly.

CHAPTER TWENTY

# PROTECTION MONEY

In the beginning he used to drive private vehicle to carry passengers. But he was tired of this job within two years as he had to give protection money to the constables and gangsters standing at different places. Whatever he earned was to be given to these gangsters.

He came to know that some government departments hired private vehicles on rent. There are some terms and conditions which have to be renewed after some definite years. But there was no tension of giving protection money to the constables and the gangsters. He purchased two vehicles with the help of some experienced people.

After one month he went to the concerned officers , filling the M.B. , to get their signature, he came to know that he had to pay some commission. If he would not give the bribe , he would not get contract in future.

Now he was compelled to compare his previous work with the present one. Previously also he had to pay money to the constable and gangsters , it was called ' Hafta ' or the protection money. Now too he has to give money to the officers which is called monthly bribe , about which no one is aware.

CHAPTER TWENTY-ONE

# WHO IS THE CULPRIT ?

Cleaning mission was at its full speed in the railway department. The employees of the sanitation department were busy in the cleaning work.

At different places on the platform shining boards were placed and on them were written in big size letters.

" Healthy environment , healthy body help us in keeping it clean "

Just then the Rajdhani express arrived on platform no.3 .A gentleman alighted from the train and he spit on the platform in discriminately.

And the board shining with 'Healthy environment, healthy body ' was completely spoiled with the tobacco juice. And it also spoiled clothes of a man passing from there , he got very angry and badly abused the railway department.

" These railway employees will never improve. See, they have not even cleaned the board." At the abuse of that passenger the board smiled satirically.

CHAPTER TWENTY-TWO

# CHANGED ENVIRONMENT

Mr Ramesh was very soft hearted and kind man. Whenever he found anyone asking for a lift or he saw anyone walking on foot , he gave the person lift on his bike and left him to the maximum possible distance.

After sometimes , he bought a car. Even though no one asked for lift , he used to take the men , women , child or young walking on foot , in his car and left them to their destination.

But suddenly everything changed.The environment became poisonous . On one summer afternoon Mr Ramesh saw a woman with her two children walking on foot in the hot summer. He stopped his car and allowed them to sit in the car .

" No, I shall not sit in your car. I can go on my own. "

With these words she moved ahead the car , which Mr Ramesh felt very strange and surprising. Suddenly he recalled the headline of the newspaper he had read in the morning , in which a car driver had misbehaved with a woman inside the car.

Mr Ramesh shivered from inside perhaps the headlines of the newspaper had compelled the lady to look him with suspicion. He decided in his mind that he would never stop his car to give lift to any woman in future.

CHAPTER TWENTY-THREE

# I KNOW THEM

Five years old Nikhil remembered his grandparents badly after he came to abroad from India with his parents. He always longed for meeting & playing the game of hide and seek with them. The innocent child , unaware of the distance , one day insisted his mother to go back to India. Mother was really confused , how to satisfy him.

An idea struck her mind. She tried to create a bad impact on his mind by criticising them , saying that they did not love him and why did he remember them and many other things

For a while he kept on listening to his mother silently then he could not control himself and spoke out.

" It's OK mother , if you want that I do not remember them or tell you to take me there , I will not. I will remember them in my mind , cry in my heart whenever I remember them but please , don't say ill of them . They are not as you are telling. They are very loving. They love me very much. I know them. "

CHAPTER TWENTY-FOUR

# ABUSE

Manoj was unable to make out why his boss was annoyed with him since last 3-4 days.

He tried to recollect his activities for last few days to find out , where he was at fault , but he was unable to find anything so finally he decided to ask his boss himself about the problem.

Reaching office, he went to the cabin of his boss and asked him the reason of his annoyance since last few days that he himself was feeling.

Boss looked at him in an angry mood but did not reveal the reason. But said , in a satirical tone.

" Oh ! how can you make a mistake. You are the successor of Harish Chandra, You never owe even a tea to anyone. ? "

Now he had understood the cause of his anger. He recalled that 3 – 4 days before he had told a contractor that in 25 years of his service, he never tried to have a cup of tea from any one , no question of bribe arises.

Perhaps this statement of mine had touched boss. In fact , I had abused him unknowingly.

CHAPTER TWENTY-FIVE

# SLAVERY

" How are you brother ? "

" Dying ! "

" Why ! "

" Sister poverty , master exploitation and criticisms always move around with me like friends. Worries always keep knocking the door. "

" It's OK from tomorrow you will get all the facilities. "

There was a light of joy in his eyes. The next day he was provided with all the facilities like --- car , bungalow , TV , fridge etc , but one thing was taken away.

After sometime there was a news in the newspaper " A man died in an A.C. room. " Everyone's attention was towards that man.

CHAPTER TWENTY-SIX

# ANEETA

He was tired of his sickness staring at the ceiling with fixed eyes but a whirlpool of thoughts was storming in his mind.

Time is so variable;everything does not happen as per our wish just like others he too thought that birth a girl child means whole life debt in the name of dowry. Thus after three sons when his wife conceived a female foetus he was very concerned and having discussed with the doctors decided to get it aborted.

While going to the doctor his wife slipped on the floor and got a fracture. It was plastered for about 45 days. Many months passed so doctors did not advise for abortion and she gave birth to her fourth child , Anita.Even after the birth of Anita his narrow-minded thinking did not change. Time passed rapidly. All the four children grew up and were married.

After retirement he fell seriously sick. Behaviour of his sons and daughters-in-law changed. Sons were busy with their office works while daughter – in – law with their children gradually they grew cruel towards him. He felt himself very helpless.

As soon as Anita got the news of her father's illness , she immediately came. She stayed for some days and served her father. But there was a little improvement. So she took him with her.

He was overwhelmed with her servitude .

He had an intent feeling of guilt.

He was thinking about the three sons who left him in his hard times , while daughter whom he tried to kill has supported him so much.

“ What would have been my condition today. If I had killed her that time. “

He kept his hand lovingly over her head and drop of tears fell from his watery eyes.

CHAPTER TWENTY-SEVEN

# ANTI CORRUPTION

Mr Arora was caught red handed taking bribe and was put in jail. He could not apply for bail also due to some legal reasons. He requested to constable to register the complaint letter , he told me about the bribe that he had to give to the C.B.I. to get it registered. Several days after he lived in the prison , C.B.I. registered the complaint letter.

Extending the copy of complaint letter to Mr Arora , the constable demanded some money once again Mr Arora's brother , standing beside gave him one thousand rupees.

The constable put the money in his pocket in front of everyone and there was no corruption team to catch him red handed.

CHAPTER TWENTY-EIGHT

# IDEALIST

" Dark age has come today. "

"What happened ? "" What has remained ? old peopleused to say , an age will come when man will snatch bread from the hand of other man. Same dark age has come today , realise it , otherwise ---------- "

" Just see , I got Balu a poor man, employed. But today his foreman has terminated him from his job "

" There must be some reason. This cannot happen without reason. " I wanted to make it clear."

" No solid reason. The foreman has employed his own man in his place. There is no law anywhere. Nepotism will never come to end in India. "

" If he is much needy, I may give him job after one month , in my section. "I said being overwhelmed with his idealism.

" Oh ! you too employ people! "

There was a gleam in his eyes.

" Then employ our Santram. "

" It's OK send him after one month. "

" After one month? "

" Yes, at present there is no vacancy. "

" Vacancy can be created. Terminate someone and employ him. What's the problem? "

" I will see. " I wanted to defer but suddenly I recalled.

" But at first you were telling about Balu! "

" Leave him yaar! Who is he not our relative? "

CHAPTER TWENTY-NINE

# INNER CONFLICT

She used to show her irritation on the small child while teaching her at night, whenever there was any hot debate in her office or tension with any of the family members. That small child had to bear all this. She used to teach her child till 1 O'clock in the night and beat him on small mistakes and beat him on small mistakes and again the same routine started at 5 O'clock in the morning till the child went to school.

The child tolerates this unexpected cruel behaviour of her mother. many times he looked at me helplessly. But my interference was more risky. She started beating him more than before. So I too tolerated all this with a heavy heart like Bhishma Pitamah tolerated the scene of "DuaupadiCheerharan."

One day I tried to convince her that she should not beat him so mercilessly. After all she is his mother. If I grow so sad. Why don't you?Don't you have any mercy in your heart?"

Resenting my words, she started weeping bitterly.

" Father I never want to beat him but what should I do ? I get too much tired in office and household work. Several times I want to leave the job but I am compelled. If his father gets a job ------- " ***

CHAPTER THIRTY

# HONESTY

Oh ! it means you have not yet seen an honest man in your life ?

" Only one , till today ---- Mr R.Mukherjee chief project manager. Really a very honest man. "

" Well, did he never accept any bribe ? "

"Why not ? he took bribe. But if he promised to do any work, he meant it "

CHAPTER THIRTY-ONE

# SERVICE WITH SMILE

As soon as the train stopped at the platform. Mr A made a survey of the platform and then entering into my coach and sat on the vacant berth just in front of me. He kept his suitcase on the seat and made a move saying that he wanted to have a talk with TTE.

So that he might get the berth reserved till Agra.

He had hardly reached a few steps on the platform when train started moving. He got into the compartment running and sat on the berth in front of me. He started noting down something in his office dairy.

" Had a talk with TTE ? " I enquired.

" He was not on the platform. Maybe he is in some coach. "

" Could you not purchase ticket ? I asked curiously.

" No, nothing like that I am railway staff. "

" Then why are you so worried ? Ticket checker would be coming after some time. "

" Actually, when you travel in a sleeper coach without reservation. It is better to inform the TTE , otherwise some of them might feel bad. "

I felt Mr A is an honest and idealist gentleman otherwise who cares. I was busy thinking when arrived the TTE.With him were three women covered in mask. He asked them to sit on the side berth which was vacant and started checking the tickets. Mt A informed that he is a railway staff and had to go Agra. At this the TTE got annoyed and said.

" You, should have taken permission ? " The gentleman took out the duty pass of first class. But the latter demanded his identity card.

" Duty pass is identity card in itself. " Said the gentleman , " But still tell me what should I show ?""

The more polite he was, the harsher the TTE was. He started abusing the gentleman and threatened to get him arrested and there would be no bail.

The gentleman explained himself again and again saying that he had gone on the platform also but he was not there. I too supported him, but TTE was not ready to listen anything and he was continuously talking nonsense. When the things went worse , the gentleman rang to someone , within moment a man came whom the TTE wished with regret.

" What's the problem Sameer ? " Asked the person who had just arrived.

The gentleman had recorded everything which he switched on and the man heard the conversation.

Stammering

" SS------- Sir, no ------ Sir, actually ----- "

"Now I have heard everything. If you can behave so rudely with our staff. What should I expect from you for the public ? Is this your service with smile ? "

The man made a move and the TTE followed him pleading.

CHAPTER THIRTY-TWO

# WELL WISHERS

His retired life was passing smoothly.Many of the works that Baburam could not complete due to busy schedule of his service, he was trying to accomplish them now. After that he felt bored lying in his room. He was thinking what to do now- daughter-in-law goes out on her job and returns by evening. Son remains busy in his business. Nobody has time for one another and grandson goes to school in morning and goes to mother's office and comes back with her in the evening, Baburam is left at home with his wife. What could they talk to each other in this old age.

I told about it to daughter-in-law, she suggested him a good idea she said , " Father it will be better for you. If you pick up Dhairya from school in the afternoon. He will come to home in time, otherwise he has to remain with me in my office till evening. He will get some time to play with you and rest for some time.

Baburamji liked the idea and from the next day he started the routine. He used to go to grandson's school in the afternoon but Mr Baburam noticed that when he returned with his grandsonsome woman from the neighbourhood used to look at him and gossiped among themselves. One day he could not stop himself and asked if they wanted to say anything.

" Nothing Babuji , actually we feel pity on you. "

" But why ? " Asked Baburam.

"Actually we have seen you since the beginning when you worked hard in your service , you never cared about the hot sun nor darkness of night.Now you are retired but still there is no peace. Your son and daughter-in-law are very cunning. They have assigned you the job of bringing Dhairya in this hot sun. "

" Thanks for your well-wishing but actually no one has assigned me this job, rather I myself enjoy the mischievous act of small children like Dhairya I am reminded of my own childhood among these children. I forget that I have become old. As far as hot sun is concerned itdoesn't bother me.

Hearing this all the ladies went inside their house , embarrassed.

CHAPTER THIRTY-THREE

# TARGET

My younger son suddenly came running and putting his hand around my neck he said, " Father, Imran's father says Allah 'O' Akbar , what should we say ? "

His innocent question arose names of many Gods and Goddesses, but I did not want to make any such imprint on his pure heart in hurry, lest he should be misguided.

I took him to the yard and asked " Dear son , can you tell me how many paths are there to climb the roof ? "

He looked at all the four flights of stairs in the four corners of the house and the wooden ladder kept there and then jumping up he said

" I got it father, I got it "

CHAPTER THIRTY-FOUR

# SELFLESS SERVICE

“What things we have to do tomorrow?” He asked his elder brother , lying covered in the Quilt.

“Tomorrow we shall clean the street in front of our house and cut wood for fuel.” Elder brother told keeping in mind the two days left for the programme.

“But brother there is no dirt in front of our house. Yes, there are many useless trees and plants in front of the house at the corner of the street. But why should we bother about it ? It is the concern of those living in that house.”

But the elder brother gave reasons “ Haven’t you seen that the house has been locked since many years.”

“Let them go why should we think about it. We have not taken contract of the cleanliness of the whole village.”

“No, contract of the country is with a single person of we should think about our house.”

That was enough.His satire touched me deeply and in the morning. I started cleaning the useless plants in front of the house that was at the corner.

CHAPTER THIRTY-FIVE

# LESSON

Sister- in-law in jeans and top in her own in law's house, advised her sister-in-law,"Listen you can't wear this salwar suit in my house. If you want to live here live properly in saree."

CHAPTER THIRTY-SIX

# FEAST

It was Ramlakhan asking for a leave just after coming back from the breakdown site.

" Why you have come just two days before from your village, Ramlakhan ? Again leave ? "

"Actually ,sir I have just got a news that my wife has fallen sick"

I passed a satire, " Oh ! just now you have come from the site. When did you get the news ?"

But he insisted again and again. I rebuked him saying"That was the reason why he could make any progress and is still on the same post even after several years why do you always lie. Tell me the truth , then only you will get leave."

He shuffled seeing my anger and said hesitatingly," shall I tell you the truth?"

" Actually, I have saved some of the poories that were distributed to us on the site. Children have not tasted poories since years. I was thinking to take it to them. "

As soon as I came to know the truth, my anger evaporated and I felt a deep sympathy for him and I agreed.

I could see a gleam in his eye as soon as I granted the leave. He tied the dry Poories of two days back and started for his village happily. ***

CHAPTER THIRTY-SEVEN

# CORONA WILL BE DEFEATED

Since morning he was busy sending messages to thousands of people on whatsapp and facebook that our PM Narendra Modi has announced that 22 March will be observed as ' Isolation Day ' to fight against corona and no one will come out of house from morning 7 O'clock till 9 O'clock at night.

He was busy reading the reactions on the mobile phone, on his post, when maid came.

He warned her saying if she did not know that P.M. has instructed every countryman to live inside their house

" No sir, I don't know "

"If you don't know then listen, you will not come out of house from tomorrow."

" But Sir, If I will not come out for work and my husband will not go for labour work, from where shall we eat ? Our earning is our daily wage. We earn some money daily and spend it. How will we live, sitting at home."

I too was worried for the house hold work. I thought, she was telling correct how will everything happen.

I was thinking all this , my daughter-in-law come out of her room saying.

" Don't worry for house chore, Seeta. We shall manage everything take this money. Arrange every necessary thing for your house today.From tomorrow no one should come out of the house. "

These words of my daughter- in- law gave me a great relief.

I was overwhelmed and said

"Corona will be defeated , corona will be defeated."

CHAPTER THIRTY-EIGHT

# COURTESY

See was murmuring in anger –

" How strange habits get formed in old age and the old people of village have gone far away from the old people of the cities. They just don't see our busy schedule and give orders to do some or other work. Wherever they want

" Give me a cup of tea " came the command although he had taken tea just an hour before.

She became furious and spoke out with anger " You are very strange Babuji. There is a timefor something. Is this your manner whenever you like you demand for a thing. I too had taken tea with you only."

The old man made a decision obeying her educated daughter-in-law.

"O, Seema ! give one more cup of tea to us."

Her husband said, who was joking and laughing with his friends.

" OK , I am just bringing." saying this she went to the kitchen to prepare tea.

Seeing this activity of his daughter-in-law the old man made one more decision.

CHAPTER THIRTY-NINE

# PUNISHMENT FOR HONESTY

This is related to a middle-class family.He earned his livelihood from agriculture with a great difficulty. He always suffered from lack of money whenever it was the time of sowing the seeds and putting manure in the field. Consequently, he has to take loan from bank.

He was born in a cultured family, hence was never dishonest so to pay back the bank loan he used to take small loans on small rate of interest and to pay back these He again took bank loans thus he was always trapped in a vicious circle of poverty. This had been continuing since many years.

During this period started election. All political parties were announcing their agenda to attract people. Along with the other farmers he too felt relief to hear that farmers loan would be excused. He too voted for the candidate who had promised to excuse the loan.

After sometimes the newly elected government conducted a meeting and fulfilled it's promise. All the farmers were very happy.

He reached the bank with his Adhar card , having completed all the other documents, he was informed that government has excused the loans of only those persons who have not paid their loans since last three years. But he repaid the loans regularly, so he was deprived of this privilege.

Everything was dark before his eyes. He was unable to understand if it was the punishment of his honesty or those people have been awarded for their dishonesty who did not repay their loans regularly.

CHAPTER FORTY

# MY OWN TURN

I was on my way from Ghaziabad to Ludhiana, two persons were sitting on the birth in front of me

" Did you see the TTE ? That bald headed. Day before yesterday he changed a penalty of 100 rupees although we are routine passengers. We travel in sleeper coach everyday nobody interferes. "

" It's obvious that the people who get their seats reserved will get more facility than the daily passengers. " One of the passengers said in a suppressed tone.

" What inconvenience? We don'tsit on his head. It's always a matter of one or one and half hours. "

The passenger became quite, guessing his attitude.

One day I had to go from Tundla to Kanpur. The train was overcrowded. Anyhow I got into a coach. After some time, I heard the roaring of a man who was abusing the daily passengers and the railway department too.

" Is this a joke ? why does the railway not make such arrangement that these daily passengers do not enter the reversed compartment. We spend our money in reservation for our comfort or to take trouble ?"

Hearing his loud roar, I too reached there. I immediately recognized him. He was the same daily passenger as I met on my way to Ludhiana. I looked at the angry passenger and said smiling.

“ Brother, why are you so angry. It’s a matter of only one and half hour, and they will get down they are not travelling on your head ? “

He looked at me angrily and recognizing me he felt embarrassed and said stammering “ Yes, yes, sit it’s a matter of only half an hour. “

The other passengers were shockingly looking at both of us turn by turn.

CHAPTER FORTY-ONE

# THE PAST

Women of the whole village had collected in the house of Ramua in Satyanarayan Katha. The priest was making preparations for the worship, surrounded by women Ramua and his wife were sitting in front of the priest when the sound of creak of laughter came from the room of Ramua's daughter-in-law all the women were shocked to hear the indecent voice.

Women started making a fuss and murmuring among themselves. Some old women could not resist themselves and spoke out " O, Ramua ! your daughter-in-law is very shameless. You say she is educated. She has no shame of neither in-laws nor village women. "

Sudha too started telling " Ramabua is perfectly right Ramua, Our daughters- in- law do not even open their mouth before their mother-in-law and sister-in-law. No question arises of speaking before father-in-law.

Ramua smiled at their gossip. Grandmother fact is that her laughter fills strength in me. So, I have told her to remain laughing.

" Have you gone mad, Ramua ? " In the whole village only you and your daughter-in-law are educated everyone else is uneducated and fools because other's daughters-in-law of the village can't behave this way."

When Ramua saw Birma Dadi becoming angry he convinced" Actually, grandmother I feel happy when she laughs. I am happy to see someone else daughter laughing. Otherwise, daughters-in-law's of others houses die suffocating inside the four walls of house. Hearing Ramua, All the women started thinking about their past.

CHAPTER FORTY-TWO

# REALISATION OF TRUTH

Many times, disaster bring a positive change in life.

Five years before my wife separated me from my family, warning me that she would commit suicide of I did not make a separate arrangement.

I tried to convince her in many ways telling her about the advantages of staying with our elders but she was firm on her resolution to leave home. I had to leave double storeyed building of my father and live on rent in a one room set.

Coronapandemic had compelled people to live confined within the four walls of the houses. So many people were dying .Everyone was in a grave fear of losing his nears and dears.

I too was much worried for my old parents, how they must be arranging everything in a lock down of months.

I was drowned in my thought of my parents when she came silently and keeping her hand on my shoulder she asked " What are you thinking Vimal ? "

" Nothing " I didn't feel it proper to share my worries with her. I was afraid if she creates a scene. So, I thought it better to keep my thoughts unrevealed.

" Vimal, don't be angry. I want to say something " I had never heard such soft tone from her. I looked at her surprisingly and asked. " Yes, tell what is your problem now ? "

I was unable to forget her behaviour of that day when she compelled me to leave my parents.

" Vimal, I want to go back to our house, and stay with my old in-laws."

I was bitterly shocked and my bitterness came out of my heart and I spoke out.

" What happened ? Is there any more drama left ? "

" You are misunderstanding me, Vimal . Corona the pandemic, which is taking away .so many lives daily has made me realise the truth of life. Everyonein the neighbourhood has lost our track since we have suffered from some cough and cold. The women of the neighbourhood, with whom I spent the whole day also did not come to ask if I need anything. "

" I passed a satire, " what about your dreams for which you left the house? "

If life is saved, we can fulfil our dream there also, Vimal. " She took a deep sigh and looked at me.

" Now I want to serve my in-laws If I am not able to do so. I can never excuse myself. "

She had realised the truth and I was gazing at her.

CHAPTER FORTY-THREE

# LAW

A man was caught for travelling without ticket. He was put in the lock up and asked twisting his ears.

"You stupid, when you had no money for the ticket and bribe then Why did you travel in the train?"

9 798887 833804

Printed by Libri Plureos GmbH in Hamburg, Germany